MW01247941

Shadowplay
2025 Issue 3

Contents

EDITOR-IN-CHIEF
Christian Chase Garner

STAFF
Christopher Bowen
Amro Eldahshoury
Kalina Smith

FACULTY ADVISOR
Mary Meriam

Cover art: Public Domain. U.S. Geological Survey. Collection: Earth As Art 5. Sources: Shuttle Radar Topography Mission. The elevation data shown here, recorded by space shuttle Endeavour in 2000, are from the Rocky Mountains of Utah and Colorado. Dark areas are low elevation, and the brightest spots are the highest elevations, here representing mountaintops.

Contact Information:
Sarah Bloom, MFA Director
phone: 870-460-1678
email: bloom@uamont.edu
University of Arkansas at Monticello
Arts and Humanities
562 University Drive
Monticello, AR 71656

https://shadowplaylit.blogspot.com
shadowplaylit@gmail.com

Shadowplay seeks work that
dances in liminal spaces, that
illuminates the pieces of our
world which otherwise go unseen.
Send us your light and your dark.

Editorial
—a cento using the works from Shadowplay *Issue 3*

this is where we live:
    an angry earth
    fracturing into
    uncountable divisions
        fear honed by
        worsening chaos
            fleeting eden
            entombed in
            a thousand kinds
            of oblivion—black
            as wet velvet

in the grief:
      believe
    in the hidden sun
        turn blackbirds
      to doves
            hurl ink
            into the void

all through
the dark—the dense
tenebris—the cobbled
light, golden and slow,
pushes through the cracks,
demanding to be seen:
    clean sheets
    wood smoke
    freezer casserole
    primordial love
    deep water sleep

milk bottles beside green dinosaurs
the sky's mooned eye
      blooming like the slender petal
      of a white flower

in this sand and anger:
    become a thing of diamond
    make a monument of mercy
    shine like light on wet side streets
    reach for it anyway
      however far you think you are
      from home

Christian Chase Garner
Editor-in-Chief of *Shadowplay*

Poems

Angelina Weld Grimké

Tenebris

There is a tree, by day,
That, at night,
Has a shadow,
A hand huge and black,
With fingers long and black.
  All through the dark,
Against the white man's house,
  In the little wind,
The black hand plucks and plucks
  At the bricks.
The bricks are the color of blood and very small.
  Is it a black hand,
  Or is it a shadow?

Suzanne Underwood Rhodes

I Imagine Old Turtle's Pilgrimage

Old Turtle's back this spring like a gift from his secret
wilderness beyond the neighbor's privacy fences,
the barking dogs, leaf blowers, delivery trucks, on past
the courthouse and funeral home, the People's Bank and First
Church of God, the prison, the pawn shop, the boarded-
up dime store, the Second Chance thrift shop. Outside time
he lumbers to the outskirts past the homeless camp
and graveyard where bluestem grasses grow and over
the hills painted in shadows, all that long, slow-going way
and from even farther he comes to stretch out his mystic neck
to drink from a Frisbee I planted in my yard as a gift to him
and all the creatures that come from someplace other
than our human place.

A Friend Giving Up in a Retirement Home
—*for Larry Richman*

You've ceased to *batter against the brilliance*
of Richard Wilbur's starling trapped in his daughter's room
as you are trapped and choose death not life in the weariness
of your failed ears, and the failed nourishment from food
or friends seated at the same plates in the same dead
air of silence spoken by strangers, the failure of books
in your shrunken room no longer companionable to save you,
books that for your whole life lit your brain—no one
had ever seen poems like yours—*the comic bones*
of incompetent beds and deep-air fishers angling
their kites upward toward the sun that even now is drawing
last year's herbs from your lonely garden to the light,
as I wish for you to find the light that loves you more than I.
It is always a matter, my darling, of life or death.
The window is open for you, God's starling.

These Corridors

When I materialize in bed
      nothing lingers
but if I keep eyes closed and breath sleep-deep
      some scrap floats up and,
           let prodding not frighten them away,
        adjacencies adhere
        a string dreamcausally connected
        and maybe another linked to the first
           only in procession
              and at the right frequency,
                interest slack enough and correctly angled,
                  odd connections accumulate

so before standing in the outside world
I wander gardens—wildernesses—of strangeness,
not seeking stories,
      eccentricity banalled by randomness,
or even, quite, details:
      the stoner neighbor I'd forgotten I remembered
      Papa alive,
           logic curled and curved
        as when the professor/surgeon said
          of my friend's brain injury
      he could no longer be squeezed
          from the same tube of toothpaste—
it's not these that make me peer
      as far down each corridor as my beam will reach.
This is where I live.
I slide my fingers beneath my wife's sleeve
chew lasagna
brake at a red light
from here.
These corridors are me.

Michelle McMillan-Holifield

Clue: Mrs. White Disappears

Her first husband was an illusionist
so there is some logic behind it

but on this occasion she's disappeared
to the movies where, by the cobbled light

of some electric trickery, she slips
through a back door and loops back home.

This is how alibies are made.
This is how bad blood turns doves

into black birds. Those omens.
She disposes of her husband. Like Kleenex.

Mark J. Mitchell

East of Sunrise

You look at what was once sand and count cars.
Their headlights cancel stars. No human face
shows through halogen glow. Yawning, you take
one step down the short stairs. A Mustang's parked,
blocking your driveway. A streetlamp cones white paint,
the safety glass windshield. You know you want
a car just like that—you drove one—your aunt's,
some cousin's. Who was the girl? She complained
that you were too slow. She wanted the speed
the car promised. You drove to a white beach
to watch moonlight on sand and hear waves and kiss
very slowly. Now, a slivered moon sinks west.
Absent dunes are pavement. Light's just a guess,
chasing dark, staying, always, just out of reach.

David Matthews

Reach for It Anyway

I peer hard into the mirror of my thought
and find there the look of a man
who would pawn his past if he could,
hurl ink into the void,
reach for venom, or vision,
desperate for poetry
that maybe never saved anyone
and not about to start now.
Reach for it anyway.

Yvonne Zipter

Requiem for a Wheel

How long had it been buried there,
in the little woods alongside Cable Lake,
the torturously twisted bicycle wheel
the excavators unearthed when they dug

the hole for our cottage's foundation?
And how did it come to its final rest
among the hickories and maples, the oaks
and buckthorns, its bent spokes huddled

around an empty hub like the slender
limbs of a daddy longlegs. Crusted in rust
and sandy soil, the wispy stems of a plant
entwined in its broken spokes, the wheel

feels somehow sacred to me, like a wooden
box or ankle bracelet unearthed at Pompeii—
the ordinary made extraordinary by time
and tumult. Garbage, is what the workmen

thought when they threw the wheel beside
the stairs. Garbage, is what my wife thought
when she saw it there. In truth, there is nothing
beautiful about this misshapen wheel.

Nevertheless, I own my reverence for it, hang it,
despite my wife's objections, on the porch
like a museum piece. Bicycle Wheel. 20th
century. Dowagiac, Michigan. Anonymous gift.

Josh Mahler

Let Me Tell You How It Started

I wake myself in my old bedroom.
A single window framing a maple tree.
See it? The realness of the leaves?

Let me tell you about fear—
the jagged limbs bending toward the glass,
rattling the pane whenever the wind

blew too hard. Never was it anything
I might call real, but as a child
it was, and this is why I remember.

It was cut down years ago, the wood
left where it fell, slowly rotting
into a dwelling for all the creatures

that forge in the safety of darkness.
Here's what you need to know—
home is two strangers that pass by

on a dirt road, nodding hello, then gone.
Home is a sweat stain on my chest,
receptacle for the heart, tool for love,

if so chosen. I'm afraid to admit it,
but the years have become memories
of the scent of wood smoke,

familiar like the trees, thick with mystery
and the secrets they guard,
like the creek coming into view,

the leaves falling like haunted eyelids,
then crushed under my feet. When I return,
I look up and thru the limbs like fingers

from an old crone casting a spell.
Another day for the sun, and I can't say
if I'll ever learn what this means.

Caleb Jagoda

Wind in the Leaves

November is so still
because the wind has no
leaves to rustle, you say.
We wind through
the graveyard,
a bounty of leaves
brittle and dead
like heaps of corpses
stiff and stagnant,
monochromatic. We've
walked this path
so many times and always
it's something different.
And there exists
so many truths
all at once: You
loving me, you trying
to love me, gravestones
ripped in two by
an angry earth,
the wind extinguishing
my cigarette again
and again. I think I never
want to see you again
but I know that's not
true. All the bodies
buried in the dirt
once bounded over it,
and now leaves
wreath the crowns
of their heads, held up
by earth—and now leaves
litter the heels of our feet,

fracturing into uncountable
divisions. A lifetime ago
they flapped in the breeze,
each an individual wing
attempting flight. But each
attached to a limb which
attached to a trunk which
sunk heavy roots deep
into the ground's guts.
And you no longer love me,
if you ever did. And the maple
behind your house refuses
to turn, steady and green,
as the cold dapples
its limbs, yanks at
its stems, as its dead
brothers loom from
all sides, emaciated
and naked. And I wonder
how many times
how many more
cold nights the maple
can take before
it decides it's not
wanted anymore.
Stubborn and green.

Susan Cobin

Breeze

This gentle breeze
is all we need—not
the soiled carrot
peelings, swirls
of evening
in the drain.

Your just washed
hair drips
down your back
leaving a trail
on the shiny
wooden floor.
You are afraid
of your reflection,
of what you might see
between the cracks.

You follow the air
like a shadow.
Your footsteps linger
in a far corner
of a garage
where a lightbulb dangles
like a loose tooth.

Andrea Potos

After a Long Day of Travel

I slept the sleep of the deep,
deep water sleep,

the deep down sleep of the dreaming
and the dead.

I slept the sleep of the underwater,
the bottomless currents of sleep

until the morning—somehow risen.
I hadn't known the depths required

to return me to the surface restored.

Daniel Weiss

Paleolithic stampede on cavern wall, Chauvet Cave, 32kya-36kya

Entombed primordial love, ochre
on the stone in the dark:
correct our fleeting eden.
You ponder as your hands work
themselves into the wall, earth
dye still hovering, speckling the
air, bloodying your flesh,
What is art but some directionless
prayer?

Signatures, corporeal shadow
makers, names overstaying their
welcome in the air and making the
tongue sore—

Spray your crimson earth on these
walls and teach us to cure our loves
with enough salt to form our own
stalactites,
long before we even consider reaching
for them again.

The dye lingers in the air and sparkles
in the torchlight—
I see your hand without you.

Moonrise over a silent earth,
but the cave still knows my touch.

Alison Luterman

July Afternoon

Not the love-making, but the afterglow. The ebb.
Clean sheets on the bed, breeze stirring the curtains.

Not the bliss, but delicious rest, when we're two canoes
moored to the same dock, bobbing in gentle backwash,

you drifting out to dream, me resisting slumber
because I don't want to miss

even a moment of this,
your long warm limbs touching mine,

hip to hip to thigh all up and down the length
of us. And what if we're already dead (I whisper,

knowing you won't hear). What if it's been a thousand years
by now, our house long gone to dust, and this spot

where we're lying is a meadow again,
dotted all over with tiny purple flowers?

A Scrap of Blue

Gray blustery day by the lake.
I'm walking to the bank,
hood up, shoulders hunched
when I pass a woman
watching the tea-colored water.
She's got that look we humans get
when we see a baby anything.
This time it's a tiny coot,
black as wet velvet,
just learning to fish, tipping head down
into the drink, then popping up again
like a cocktail glass ornament.
I wouldn't have seen it on my own,
striding blindly as I always am,
fighting the elements,
fighting late-stage capitalism
and losing. But I could ride
the coattails of her attention
for a moment, could notice
her noticing and so slip
through a crack between
the thousand kinds of oblivion. A scrap
of blue when clouds part
just enough. In twelve step programs
they say you have to be willing,
but if you're not, then perhaps
you might be willing to be willing,
and so on, until finally some kind of light
may find even you, however cranky
and rain-splattered, however far
you think you are from home.

Whitney Cooper

Echoes of a Creekside Mill

Stone walls neatly stacked,
roofless mouth   missing
teeth. Wooden stakes board
any openings as if to keep out

any youthful stupidity.
Once home to Confederate paper,
the mill survives Union fire.
Water weeps   from the sides

of the rock wall and tumbles
          into the creek. The creek's rushing
body rolls back over the bank, over
the South's bloody

indignation. I am afraid   to look,
to consider the beauty
of this place. Home is the roar
of the creek, stones stabbing

through wet, violent clay.
My South, in its sweet   summer swelter.
I break this bread with a copperhead,
who   awakens from its sleep

under the mill wall and coils
its amber body deeper
into the   solemnity of the woods.
I dream flames have licked this place clean.

Ron Riekki

She says, *I worship the sun*

when I ask her
if she believes in God
and I've never met her,
will never meet her,
this woman I met online,
who called me
and talked about the sun
the entire call,
an hour,
where all she talked about
was the sun
and I wanted to see
if she could sustain it,
and she could,
talking about how
it's a star
and how she loves
the stars,
and that word—*love*—
kept glowing
into the conversation,
not about me,
but about the metabolic processes
of a planet that—*no!*
she interrupts, *no!*
the sun is not a planet!
and she's so adamant,
so passionate,
and talks about A.A.
and I feel surprised
that the sun has burnt out
and we've moved on,
but she says, no,

that in A.A.
they forced her
to acknowledge a higher power
and that she didn't believe in God,
but she believed in the sun,
so she let the sun
be her God
and the sun helped her to get sober
and I ask,
clarify,
Are you talking about your son?
As in, like, a daughter?
And she says,
The sun is my daughter
and I am the sun's daughter,
and she uses the word *oblateness*
and I think she's a genius
and mad
and OCD
and good
and lost
and wise
and weird
and I'm hooked
and on guard
and we're talking at night,
late at night,
which is when I meet all people,
when the sun is sleeping,
and she's wide awake
and I ask her if it's hard
that she can't look at
the thing she loves
and she tells me
that, no, she has glasses
to see the eclipse
and never misses the eclipse
and I tell her I love the moon

and she says,
If we ever fuck,
I think it will end the world
and I'm so lost at this line
and so charmed by this line
and so confused by this line
and she says she has to go
and I say something and she says, no,
she really has to get going
and she hangs up
and I go to the window
look up,
searching.

Belly

I am lying still and holding my belly in my hands. I
am trying to hold myself together by holding
myself. I am trying to catch myself before I fall
over and my insides fall to the ground. I hold
myself together by holding myself.

My belly is soft and round, swollen with indecision
and promises yet to be fulfilled. I am unable to feel
the warmth I know is inside me. I am unable to
touch, but I can hold, so I hold.

I hold myself together with hands that are too
swollen to grasp, knotted with arthritis, useless to
do anything but hold. My breath comes in long,
drawn movements. No sudden changes. There is no
storm over this ocean, only the roll of steady wave.

It would be so easy for the tide to pull me apart. To
separate limbs, spread fingers, pluck each hair from
body, loosen teeth from gum line. The water takes
not only breath, but strength. But I can still touch
my hand to belly. I can still hold myself. I can still
hold myself together. I can still hold myself.

Stasha Cole

kitchen witches

while today he poured the
beeswax we salted the grind
herbed potion uncomplete
without wild unrefined
why is the rhyme caught in the teeth
thyme sought in the grief
what's a casserole in the freezer
but love on hold

Emma Bolden

Inside the Sibyl's Silence

What is the body but a hinge
of breath that opens to the living,

closes unto death. Inside my body's
architecture an end has already found me.

I cradle it, a robin's skull
against my breasts. Long ago I grew

proud to call myself witch,
my every word a red

contusion blooming. What a gift,
to hold bitter as sincerely

as sweet beneath the tongue.
I can offer no words that mean

to understand. What a crimson
beauty I still see in myself, in my

own inscrutable focus, as tight
as the sky's mooned eye.

Redshift

O far bright, o last
        long, o longing
was the window through which I
        watched the world
ode its wants, a hum I could
        never fit in my throat.
Inside myself absence lived
        as the presence of need: more
beauty, more egg shell
        cracked open to reveal
its hidden sun, more
        the morning dressed
in drawn drapes &
        the grass tonguing green
a gray stripe of sky &
        the incessant wonder of
a body shifting through
        its words & what I know
already: there is a whole in me,
        an empty I love as the only
thing I & alone own.

Megan Leonard

A Love Song to the Generations, with Mercy

The mother trauma, the woman trauma,
it shakes down like armloads of sand. It was heavy
at the outset, but now
just sticks to everything, can't be undone,
the memory of shoreline gritting everything,
peppering the bottoms of feet,
rasping the kitchen floor and the soft planks
in the narrow hallway.
We sweep the sheets out with wide palms
before making the bed, but it makes no difference.
Shake the shoes   and tap them on the heels,
but the sand still shows up between toes,
under fingernails, on the scalp and in hair.
A witch, accused, imprisoned, set to hang.
A ghost, kidnapped from her home, enslaved, turns herself into a vision.
Their children and children's children twine with
sand and anger and the weight of sand and the baby that becomes me
takes her first breath with a rasp and a rough foot,
heel torn up like paper.

I was my mother at the start of the year

At the start of the year, I was cutting camellias which smell like nothing,
but not in the same way snow does. Fresh snow's nothing
is the something of everything else around it: burnt gasoline
from Joann's truck and the dirt her sliding wheels exposed.
Inger Christensen tells us,

> *add*
> *words, but let*
> *things be; see*
> *how easily they find*
> *shelter by themselves.*

See, at the start of the year, Joann was a woman without a license
driving to a bar in Flint that closed ten years ago. Her last winter made
a question of each of us. Sometimes when I called she'd go, who are you?
but other times she would tell me who I was. She did not remember
she didn't have a granddaughter, so at the start of the year I was my brother,
my uncle, someone I'd never heard of. I borrowed these lives that let me
meet her at the end of hers, slipped into them like another man's shoes.
Most days, everyone was my mother. I was my mother the last time we spoke.
My mother's mother said I love you and as my mother I said goodbye.

Emma Johnson-Rivard

The Poet Writes a Ghost Story

Years before, the gift of muse became a radiant lens
born to a young lesbian. These are interesting times.

What is the lie? It weighed her relationships to
women, food, consumption, and bones—all of it
into a kind of perfectionism and fierce poetry.

Her sentences became hills, her ghosts a mountain.
It's no wonder she wrote such brutal tales in unwitting lands.
Her arrival became a tinderbox. She can survive anything.
In sure hands, reincarnation becomes a thing of diamond.

Jeffery Allen Tobin

What the Light Does

All afternoon, it slides across the floor,
golden and slow, touching everything—
the chair where you sat reading,
the glass left half-full on the table,
the thin blue vein on the back of your hand
when you reached for nothing in particular.

Even now, the light finds its way in,
a thin blade slipping between
the window frame and the hush of evening.

What does it want?
To make a monument of dust,
to bless the ordinary,
to remind us—softly,
without urgency—
that we are already disappearing.

Jan Freeman

Refrain

This is the cage I call my body
This is the cage I call my home
Under the lines of shade and shadow
breath is my metronome
Absent of shade, absent of shadow
intonations are my bones
What I remember, all I forget
hard and soft, my fear was honed

Cliff Saunders

My City of the Lone Whistle

My mind has warped into
six lanes of worsening chaos.
Drunk, asleep, I bask
in the swing rhythms of spring.

It's no wonder I love sleeping
outdoors near the beach.
After all, I am a survivor of religion
and fast cars, sex in heaven

or beer in hell—all of it.
As free as a wild sense
of wonder, rain falls on stormy
waters, on crumbling roads

that keep getting lost. Why is it
raining through *these* fingers?
I believe with all my heart
that the shadow on a seawall

is a huge amen. Let us pray.
The chipping away whips up
whirlpools block by block,
day by day. Out of my way,

life I pictured when the world
went dark. Let the stars align
as they shine on wet side streets.
This is my city of the lone whistle.

At this rate, the swirling wind
will be lost to quiet doubt
no matter what people hang
from atop a cosmic shrine.

And the rest, as they say,
is feeling the love, the loss,
the dissemination of hope
in all its haphazard glory.

For my Children

The farther away we move away from there
the more I feel it, the suburbs of the city of your wound,

the wound I dealt, the city I built,
a dense, collapsed-star place of no place,

a presence of absence, abandonment.
I abandoned you, sitting right in front of you,

I abandoned you, passed out in my bedroom.
I nearly left you completely, one night,

as surely as by predator or accident.
It was an accident. No one plans this.

And it is better, now, recovery, me, us.
I am covering old territory again, for sure,

again, I am remembering as I couldn't
in the midst of it, I am remembering

as if quite literally re-member-ing
a body blasted to bits by a bomb.

Health, healing, again.
Movement in, and of, life, again.

Still I know that small endless darkness
in you, that damage, abyss,

I, your mother, put in you. I am here, now,
telling you this, I am here.

Michael Milburn

Ask Away

I had them
write down
everything they
could think of

they could lose,
and what they'd
most/least like
to live without.

I got homework, parents,
mornings, phones,
little brothers (pro and con)
and from one girl, her period,

which was modern, I thought.
No father of daughters,
I'd never heard anyone
I wasn't married to

say it quite like that.
No groans or chuckles from the boys,
as if progressive parents
and a progressive school

in a progressive state
added up to a twelve-year-old
naming it out loud
to zero mockery.

Only the arrested
adolescent in me
was shocked to hear
a word so bold, defiant,

indignant, intimate,
plaintive, proud,
sincere, helpless,
shrewd, and true.

Sherry Abaldo

Are there any more showgirls on the Las Vegas Strip or are they all just street performers? **the tourist asked.**

One man says *You're not real.*
I say *Not real what?*
One man says *My grandmother
was a showgirl – 5'10", a ballerina,
a goddess, your problem is
you are not unattainable.*

One man pays 50 bucks for a
photo of me and Estrella in a
sandwich with his 10-year-old son.
Pink sequins on our tits leave zit
like marks on his face. Later I mace
a drunk thug, he pukes on my boots.

My mother says *I've had a broken
heart longer than you've been
alive.* Buys me Tylenol, face
roller, cellulite cream, fishnets,
bottle of Jack Daniels Black,
begs me to be a nurse.

My mother says *Heavy lies
the head that wears the crown*
when she's drunk, which is
when she's breathing. My red
headdress leaves a slow ache of
weight like an anti-halo.

Someday I will break this curse.
Somebody will toss me a magic
coin. One man tells me about
Paris, the *Folies,* the dusky river,
the bread and the wine and the
lights, the woman he lost.

Fiction

Good Evening, My Friend

The weekend after Gabe got fired from the auto repair shop for accidentally causing an electrical fire, he took a Greyhound up to Albany to see his grandfather at the memory care center. The moment he'd been dreading for the past three years had finally come—his grandfather didn't recognize him anymore. "Don't take it personally," the nurse said, as if that was supposed to make him feel any less depressed about the situation.

When Gabe got home, he hopped into the shower and attempted to wash away his streak of motor oil and misery. He squeezed out a glob of shampoo, more than he intended, and it slid off his palm and splattered onto the porcelain. "Money down the drain," he thought to himself.

He tip-toed out of the bathroom and into his cramped box of an apartment. Rusty nail heads protruded from the wooden floorboards like mushrooms. Going barefoot in that place was to play a game of fate with tetanus. The stench was putrid. Mice would steal crumbs of food, and cockroaches were roommates who didn't pay rent. All the critters gave him the shivers, but he didn't have the heart to kill them.

After eating a bowl of stale cereal for dinner, Gabe crawled into his creaky bed and stared at the water-stained ceiling. His world felt a lot more empty, and his walls felt a lot more suffocating. He couldn't stop thinking about the state of his grandfather. *Maybe next time he'll know who I am,* he hoped. *Or maybe he won't. Maybe the time after that he will. Or maybe he won't.* Then Gabe began to ponder if there would even be a next time.

Just then, he heard the sound of a screech out on the balcony. He looked through the window and saw two yellowish eyes piercing the shadows. The glow of the city lights revealed a speckled coat of brown feathers and a pair of antenna-like ears that stood at attention. "An owl," he whispered. Perched upon the balcony's railing, it was the most exquisite creature he'd ever seen. Before he had the chance to exhale his halted breath, the owl flew off into the deep violet sky.

The following night, Gabe heard the screech again. His eyes widened and his heart raced as he leaped out of bed. The owl had returned to the balcony. It had its back turned to the window. "Good evening, my friend," he whispered. The owl slowly turned its head all the way around and locked eyes with him. It was a glare that was as wise as it was curious, and as calming as it was intimating. He recalled how his grandfather told him that seeing an owl means good luck. And off it went.

The owl continued to make an appearance on the balcony every night, until the night that it didn't. *Maybe tomorrow,* Gabe thought. He would stay awake until his eyelids got heavy, but the owl never showed. One day, Gabe concocted a plan to lure one of the mice from his apartment into a plastic container and use it as bait. It was his hardest, sweatiest job since he had work. When the sun set, he placed the container with the mouse in it out on the balcony and waited all night for the owl to swoop in. But the owl was nowhere to be seen. By the time the sun rose, he'd accepted that the owl wasn't coming back.

The next day, he used the remaining money from his last paycheck to purchase a Greyhound ticket and go see his grandpa up in Albany again. *Maybe when I tell him about the owl, he'll remember me,* he thought. *Or maybe he won't.*

The C Sign

"Cunt!" Andy's voice called, evaporating into asphalt heat.

"Cocksucker!" I countered. I leaned on the already-leaning, rusted signpost for "C PARKING." No signs for A, B, D, or beyond in sight.

"Coward!" his voice neared.

"Chump." I kicked the C sign. Andy handed me his bottle of strawberry seltzer, and I sucked a gulp down. He pulled a pack of grape gum from his pocket while we walked through the weed-busted lot toward the old factory or warehouse or whatever it used to be but wasn't anymore and never would be again. I hoped our bikes would be ok dumped in the bushes. No one bugged them last time.

I handed Andy back the bottle and he swigged, picked up a rock, hurled it toward the huge wall of concrete blocks and vines and mostly-obliterated windows, but we were too far away still for it to hit. His shoulder bumped mine, and I stepped a step away as we walked. I swore I wasn't going to kiss him this time.

"I suppose they'll all be smashed-out eventually," he said, and the windows glinted steel cloudcover and flashes of sun. There were never any birds.

"Guess so." I said.

"Your sister ok?"

"Don't know yet," I said, and I chucked a hunk of asphalt toward a window pane. Its shatter was disappointingly quiet in the hot afternoon whirr of crickets and wind and nearby highway truckdriving rumbles. "Mom's had the phone in her lap for two days."

"I left the cards here," Andy gestured toward the building's old doorway. No doors anymore. A chipmunk streaked away from the shrubby weed mess inside what must've been a lobby, and we sat on our two concrete blocks. Andy handed me the seltzer while he pulled the deck of cards from a Ziploc bag stuffed in a Folgers coffee can stuffed in a tire stretched and crackled in a C shape.

I sipped while he dealt, tasting his upper-lip sweat on the spout along with the strawberry. I wanted it to rain. The air seemed to want to rain.

"I de-clare war," we chanted, each slipping our four cards on the concrete block between our knees. My queen beat his nine and I scooped up the cards. He grumbled. I scanned the clouds, smelled distant dampness in the heat of the air like a laundromat or the locker room at the Y. If it rained, our bikes would be wet riding home, tires spitting mudpuddle water up our backs. My sister would watch the rain run down the window from her bed in thin wormy rivulets that would just keep streaming down and down and down.

"...war," we said, and my left knee touched his right, and I let it because it felt like tiny lightning. Andy handed me the last swig of the bottle. I finished it, leaning my neck way far back. Then I flung the bottle much harder than I needed to into a shadowed corner of what used to be two reliably solid walls.

·

Tracks

A family holiday up in Canada at Shuswap Lake, that's how Nate had pitched it, the girls would love it, a beautiful place he went to as a boy to swim and fish and do nothing. But as they drove up here, Gretta saw lots of bear warning signs. Watch out, and now, in the morning, the wet dirt in front of the cabin was covered in bear tracks, more than a dozen, as if the animal spent the night pacing and plotting and planning. Tracks the size of a big man's hand.

Charlotte, who was seven, stood next to Nate, bug-eyed, but Little Bella, bold and unflinching and innocent, bent down and poked her pudgy finger into a print, making a divot in the dirt.

"Don't," said Nate. "They're going to get your smell and come find you and eat you all up."

He said that last part in a playful voice, but he could never fully erase that thumped-up authority. One day here, his face was stubbled, and his curly black hair was frizzy because of the hard water. Gretta thought that resounding authority was built into the male voice, and Nate got an extra dose. Bella, with her two pigtails jetting out and her big baby belly, clung to Gretta's shorts. Tall, skinny Charlotte was working hard to keep her big girl face. Their vacation stood in the long shadow of bears, hungry bears, big bears, bears that mauled. Look, a pile of bear scat, which resembled people poop, only black.

Tears streamed down two-year-old Bella's chubby baby cheeks as if she was imagining a bear hunting her down and gobbling her up.

"Oh, come on, now," said Nate. "Be a big girl."

Gretta whispered in her ear not to worry, she'd watch for the bears.

"Why don't you go down to the lake and look for minnows," she said. Because they were supposed to be on vacation and all this talk of bears, well, it was frightening Gretta, too. She was always the one who had to provide the counterbalance to Nate's gruffness. She was the one who smoothed things over and calmed everyone down with light and levity. Lately, she'd grown tired of it.

Bella's eyes brightened and she made a waddling beeline for the lake. Yesterday, she had happily scooped up fish in a cup and poured them out again, mesmerized by the waterfall dotted with tiny sparkling silver. Gretta had gone to the lake with Bella and tried to read her book—though most of the time she watched Bella to make sure she didn't fall in or get mauled by a bear. Nate sat on the deck and taught Charlotte how to whittle, first a stick, then a block of balsa wood. Not long after that, Gretta found herself pounding nails into the wobbly picnic table—Nate's latest project. He had Bella and Charlotte use sandpaper to smooth out the tabletop. By late afternoon, it was warm enough to swim, and Nate lifted squealing Charlotte and tossed her in the water, her head popping up like a seal in the dark lake, shouting, "Do it again, Daddy!" Gretta stayed near Bella, who wore floaties and kicked her chubby legs, chasing luminescent blue dragonflies.

Gretta went to the front porch and stretched out on a lawn chair. Perfect weather, the sun burning off the mist and light falling all over the tree branches. She needed some time for herself. When she packed for this vacation, in a fit of silly delusion, she brought four books. If she read a page today, she'd be lucky. She moved her bare legs, so they were in the sun, hoping to tan them. George had called them delicious. They'd all gone out after work to Hal's Bar, all the reporters, and she was included, though she was only a part-timer. Her work was nearly meaningless, writing little stories about a store closing, a wedding, or an event at the town hall, but she loved it, and who knew she might have a future there. All that excitement in the newsroom, the clatter of the keyboards, phones ringing, interviews, sharp exchanges. George had had a little too much to drink and got friendly in that talkative way. She'd laughed and that encouraged him to say more. She didn't mind. How easily he laughed, how she laughed so easily.

There went Nate, marching down to the lake with an

armful of chopped wood, Charlotte following behind him like an obedient puppy. Oh, how much she wanted his attention and love, it was heartbreaking. He was a man who had a purpose. He could not, for the life of him, be idle. She'd once loved that about him; his bottomless energy, his drive; he planned outings and vacations, and he'd always be a good provider. But he'd promised on this vacation, everyone would relax. But then again, she reminded herself, he also said he wanted to teach everyone practical things. He wanted his daughters to be capable and confident, not flimsy sidekicks that the world battered around. You can be anything, he'd tell them, but it was baffling to Gretta because he had a different attitude toward her. Why did she have to get a job? Running around town as a reporter, my god. He made more than enough money, and what she earned went straight to the babysitter. How did that make any sense? "Let me answer that," he said. "No."

"Come on down here," Nate shouted to Gretta. He'd taken the wood to the lake and piled it on the rocks. Today's lesson was about building a fire. Gretta sighed, glanced at the woods, where she was sure a bear or whatever wild animals were out there would emerge. It seemed like, given all the warnings, someone should stand watch. In truth—how terrible to acknowledge—she'd like to finish this chapter, a story about two runaways on a train, but she found herself putting her book down and going to the lake, her legs warm from the sun.

They set to work collecting small sticks, Bella, too, and she put them in her cup. "They're called kindling," said Nate, then he had Charlotte repeat it, which irritated Gretta. Talking down to the girls and to her, as if they and she knew nothing, as if she and the girls were empty vessels, and his purpose, his job was to fill them up. The big wood goes on top of the kindling, he said. Gretta bit the inside of her cheek. She couldn't say when all his little quirks and ways became so exasperating to her. At the bar, when George had reached over and moved a strand of hair from her cheek, a warm little thrill ran through her. He playfully, drunkenly said she should change her name to something more glamorous. Genevieve, maybe.

He rattled on, saying they should start a magazine, something wild, bizarre, crazy.

Light the match to the kindling, Nate told them. The fire refused to obey. Only one stick glowed, smoldered, and sputtered out. He had to light another match, another, all the while muttering profanity, but finally, one stick caught, then a big log sparked and flamed, and the girls shrieked with delight.

Dusk came drifting in and the last light turned pink and peach. The girls stood beside her, watching the astonishing light and the ducks. "It's so beautiful," said Gretta. When the wind picked up, rippling the surface of the lake, they went inside. Gretta told the girls that tomorrow they'd bake a chocolate cake.

"And then we'll eat it all up," said Charlotte, sneakily glancing at Nate. Gretta smiled at her, her smart Charlotte with her jab at Nate, turning his words back on him. He didn't hear her, or pretended not to hear.

In bed that night, Gretta pictured a bear stalking the cabin, trying to find a way in. If it could smell as well as Nate said it did, it would smell the food in the kitchen. The house was sleeping, Nate was snoring, but Gretta couldn't slip into a dream. She got up and checked the doors and windows. When she peeked outside, she thought she saw the glow of two orange eyes the size of marbles right at the edge of the woods. They seemed to be looking right at her. And then they vanished as if she wasn't supposed to see them, as if it was a rip in the seam of the possible that wasn't meant for her.

In the morning, Nate announced today was the big day, fishing day. They'd learn to fly fish. The girls said in a sing-song voice they wanted to fish for flies, and Gretta laughed, so the girls kept singing it. Happiness floated through the air, and the sun was out again. Nate left for the town to buy bait and came back with a container full of red wiggling worms that, to Gretta, looked like a seething ball of anger. Bella asked if she could pretty please have one, and before Nate could answer, Gretta said of course. Bella gently picked one up and, holding it in her palm, took it outside, talking to it the whole time.

They went down to the lake, a parade, Nate leading the way with the fishing poles and Charlotte carrying the bait as if it was an offering. They stood in a row in the lake on either side of Nate, who showed them how to take the pole behind their heads and then forward again, quickly, rapidly, like throwing a ball. Bella tried and accidentally threw the pole in the water. When she did it again, Gretta told her it was fine, don't worry, but Bella didn't want to do it anymore. She went over to the other side of the dock with her cup.

They practiced without fishing line or bait, and soon, the girls were hungry. Gretta went up to make sandwiches and lemonade. She scanned her phone, looking at the headlines of the *Times Beacon,* and saw George had written about the Board of Supervisors and the six-hour budget negotiations, which meant he was up all night. When she checked her texts, there was one from George: *when r u coming back????* She smiled and remembered how, after he'd moved the strand of hair from her face, he'd stood, and when he didn't come back right away, she followed his path and found him outside in the back. He kissed her hard. He was her height and wore black glasses and had a master's degree in literature. In the newsroom, she heard him speak to his mother in Czech. She read his text again, feeling her face turn hot, then quickly deleted it.

Suddenly shouting, Charlotte was shouting for her, "Mommy!" and Gretta raced outside, picturing a bear lunging for her daughter.

"We saw a bear!" she said, pointing to the shore. A black bear had ambled down to the water to get a drink. "I saw it! It was big!"

Nate looked like he'd won an argument. Bella whined that it wasn't fair because she didn't see it and wanted to.

"It might come back, you wait," said Nate.

As Nate added fishing lines and hooks to the pole, Gretta sat on the warm rocks, knees drawn up to her chin, and listened to the lapping water. They'd leave soon, she thought, and as she picked up her book, wondering if George might text her again, something sharp stung her cheek and it all seemed to happen at once, the sting yanked her up from the ground, hauled her toward the water, dragged her into the water, and the pain in her cheek, and the girls were screaming and she was screaming, the lake tossing the high alarm into the blue air. Something dripping down her face, the sting took her straight to Nate, who rushed toward her and yanked out the hook.

The girls solemnly took her hand, and they walked back to the cabin, which was so dark and dank, like entering a cave. Gretta could barely see. They led her to the couch and sat beside her, so close as if to protect her. Charlotte put her hand on Gretta's leg, telling her she'd be alright.

The hook went in a quarter inch below her right eye. Nate insisted they go to the hospital for stitches. On the way back, he said in that low voice. "I told everyone, never stand behind someone who is fly fishing. Never never never."

That was a long time ago, and so was the marriage, which ended for many reasons. Gretta lives in an apartment in San Francisco and works for *The Guardian,* covering art, film, and books. Her daughters are young women, confident and capable, who hold only wispy vestiges of that trip: bear tracks, bear sightings, the smell of bear scat. Though they know it's not true, it couldn't be, but when they see the scar on their mother's cheek, their first thought is that a bear did it. When they were girls, that's what they told their friends.

"I was so worried a bear would come into the cabin," says Charlotte.

"Me, too," says Bella.

When the light hits Gretta's cheek at a certain slant, the scar shines brightly and looks like a tear, as if she's crying. Sometimes, someone asks if she's OK, and she tells them, "I tangled with a bear." She's fine, she assures them, absolutely fine.

Memorial Drive

Abby boarded the Marta bus at Midway, traveling up Memorial Drive, and she sat down in front of me. Robert was with her, and they were wearing matching ball caps. She didn't acknowledge me because a third guy I didn't know was with them. I played along.

They were loaded up with grocery bags. Abby operated at the Walmart back on the other side of Midway where they got on board. Most days, with a little cardboard sign, she would get lines of people in cars handing her dollar bills. If it wasn't for the drugs she would be making a fortune. She was young and cute, and God only knows she must have a miserable father somewhere back in Louisiana where she came from.

I'd ride my bike on a ten-mile loop from Decatur, down to the Beltline and back. She'd be standing there with her little sign, and I wouldn't give her money, but I'd deliver a clam-shell boxed salad from Walmart. I think everything else she ate came from vending machines. Sometimes I would bring Strawberry Twizzlers because she liked them—not the Pull n Peels ones, nor the short ones, and nothing but Strawberry. Never money. I have a daughter in New Mexico.

When we halted at the Beech Drive stop, they were profusely thanking the guy for the food, telling him how hard it was for them. That part was true. They lived in a tent behind the mausoleum, and it was excruciatingly expensive to keep up a drug habit.

Before we got to the Bobbie Lane stop Abby spoke to the third guy I didn't know, "I need that piece of paper in your hand so I can write down your name so we can pray for you," she said. It was the receipt for the groceries.

The guy I didn't know looked like he was surprised by everything. He gave her the receipt and exchanged hugs with them before he got off at the Covington Drive stop. As soon as the bus started up again, they rustled around getting their bags ready to disembark at the next stop. That was Highway 278 where there was a nice open area and a good walkway to get back across Memorial. That's where they could catch the next Marta bus in the opposite direction—with their groceries, and with their receipt. They would need that for the refund.

Apokalypsis

Sandra stared out the window onto the street below. From four stories up the world was peaceful. Traffic flowed in neat silent lines. Just enough daylight to identify individual vehicles. But not the one that mattered.

"Mrs. Bennett?"

If his car pulled up in the next seven minutes, Sandra told herself, there would be time. Maybe even six minutes if they hurried.

"Mrs. Bennett, are you ok?" asked the lawyer. "Can I get you a seat?"

Sandra nodded, wondered if it were a standard courtesy to a woman in her condition or if the lawyer could sense her anxiety. She allowed him to help her into a chair. It took the pressure off her lower back she hadn't realized she'd been carrying.

"I'm sorry," she said after the worst of the nausea had passed. "I don't know that he's coming."

"We still have a few minutes," said the lawyer. "Maybe he'll get here."

It had been two days since she had seen him or communicated in any way. The odds were growing long that he'd suddenly materialize in the next few moments.

Sandra's phone buzzed in her pocket. There it was. Kurt's number.

"Kurt!" she blurted into the phone. "I'm here! At the lawyer's office!"

"I don't know how long I've got," said the voice on the other end.

"For God's sake, where are you? Please don't tell me you got lost again..."

"I don't know how long I've got," Kurt repeated. "Frankly, I'm shocked that I've got a signal at all – it's the first I've had in days. Must be heighted magnetic activity from the event. I guess that's a good sign?"

The words were coming out in that rapid-fire manner he used when excited.

"Kurt, the lawyer!" she repeated.

"Oh. That's today?"

Sandra stifled a scream.

"I thought that was next week. Must have put the wrong date in the calendar," said Kurt.

"Is that your husband, Mrs. Bennett?" asked the lawyer.

"We've got to sign the papers in the next five minutes," said Sandra. "Five minutes, Kurt! Otherwise we're going to lose the sale!"

"The sale? Sandra.....it doesn't really matter. Where I am, what I'm about to experience, it's so much more important than that."

Sandra took a moment to compose herself. She couldn't lose control right now. Kurt didn't operate like that. He was remorselessly logical.

"I need you to get in the car and drive down to the lawyer's office," she stated in a reasonably level tone. "Whatever else you have planned, we can discuss it when you get here. Only you need to get here *right now.*"

There was a moment's pause, enough to make Sandra worry that the call had dropped.

"I can't do that," he said. "I'm not in the area. Technically not even in the country."

"Kurt," she half shouted, half moaned into the phone, "what are you talking about?"

"My god, Sandra! Remember the thing I was telling you about? It's about to happen! I'm going to be here to see it first-hand. First human in at least seven hundred years at least. Possibly ever!"

The blood drained from Sandra's face.

"No, you don't mean…"

"I finished the calcs on Monday and realized it was coming right away," Kurt explained, his words rushing together. "I mean, right away. There was literally no opportunity to call, pack a bag, anything. I had to leave that instant or miss my window. It was chaos. The flights, charter, car, the boat...."

"Where is here!?"

"Thirty-nine degrees, twelve minutes, ninety-nine seconds latitude, seventy-six degrees, ninety minutes, sixty-one seconds longitude."

"Kurt, I don't...."

"Wait—scratch that. I reversed the lat long. I'm on a boat about, uh, seven nautical miles off the west coast of Greenland. Pretty rough chop but perfect visibility. Cloudless night. Couldn't ask for better. Not that I think that will matter much if this goes the way I think it's going to."

"We *can't* lose this sale," Sandra pleaded. "There's no other option, Kurt. There's no place left for us to go."

"I know," he said. "I figured we'd lose the co-op if I did this. I guess I didn't really care."

Whatever last reserve of hope she'd been holding onto crumbled. Three years of suppressed grief poured out of her in hot, sticky tears. The savings and the fights, the unrelenting stress. The times she had physically broken down and willed herself back. All of it in service to this moment where the payout was within reach...

The lawyer looked uncomfortable at the display of emotion. He stared on impotently.

"We're homeless, Kurt! Don't you understand?" Sandra sobbed. "The lease has lapsed on the apartment. Until we get the co-op deposit back, we can't afford another. That's all the money we have in the world. My money, Kurt, as you seem to have checked out on your job."

"About that," said Kurt. A pause. "I had to use that downpayment to finance this trip. But it's totally going to be worth it because...."

Sandra put the phone down. Kurt wasn't lying because Kurt didn't lie. She now had a totally new crisis to deal with.

"Mrs. Bennett, it's now seven-fifty-eight pee-em," the lawyer interjected. "In two minutes I'm legally obligated to end negotiations and inform the seller that the deal's off."

She ignored him and put the phone up to her ear, realized that Kurt was still talking.

"...in its wake, will produce a gravitational ripple that right-shifts electromagnetic waves so dramatically that background radiation undergoes an aurora effect and may even push sounds into the visible spectrum. What's most exciting is the coronal lensing, which is going to create unprecedented opportunities for astronomical observation. We ought to have a clear sightline all the way to the edge of the universe and even a window into the past, possibly as far back as the singularity. But really, there's not even a theory of what this thing is going to feel like. My model shows..."

"Shut up!" she snarled. "I don't care about this! All this time I've been killing myself trying to pull this together for us, for our family, you were planning to run off on some selfish trip to see the northern lights, or whatever..."

"The Celestial Period," he interjected. "Or, the Vacuous Apparition. Still not sure what I'll end up calling it. Which do you like better?"

"You abandoned us Kurt. I hope you can live with that. You miserable fuck."

The last expletive stuck in her throat, didn't land with the impact that she had intended.

"I don't know that I have to. Live with it, I mean," said Kurt. "This is an untested cosmic force. Even if I do survive the experience, there's not an easy way back home. I'm almost out of fuel. Got enough to idle here for twenty minutes then I'll just drift. Maybe someone will pick me up. But I haven't seen any other boats."

The lawyer appeared to have lost interest in her conversation. He was standing over at the window squinting up at something on the other side. Frowning. There was an odd light filtering through the window, a dark red glow like the inside of a volcano. It gave his face a devilish shine.

"When I considered the consequences, the opportunity to witness this event was greater than the guilt of ruining your life," said Kurt. "If I'm being honest, this obsession you had with the co-op, raising a family....I guess I never really understood it."

Sandra slid out of the chair, down to the floor.

"If you only knew what this experience was going to be," said Kurt, "you'd have done the same. People would sacrifice everything, throw it all away to see this just one time. It's just that they don't know. Can't know. I mean, how can you possibly explain it?"

"...but you didn't..." she mumbled.

"What's that? I didn't hear you."

"You left me alone to deal with..." She took a breath. "Maybe I don't want all of this this either. But you didn't give me the chance. But you didn't *take* me."

"There wasn't time," he explained, softly.

There was a noise like a cat chattering at a bird. Sandra looked back at the window. The lawyer's mouth hung open, eyes glazed over, a strand of drool running down his chin. Whatever was happening to him, she couldn't spare the effort to care.

"I'm going to hang up the phone now," Sandra said with the last of her strength. "I know this has been a difficult conversation and this may be the last time we speak, so I'm going to choose my words carefully..."

"Hold up, don't go! We're just ten seconds away," Kurt said. "Stay on the line at least until this starts. I'll describe it as long as I can. Won't you stay on?"

There was a crash. Sandra turned just in time to see the lawyer's foot disappear through the shattered window.

"Any second now," said Kurt.

The metallic thud of a car collision rang out from the street below. An inhuman scream coming from somewhere outside. The reddish light had begun to flicker and slow down. But that wasn't quite right. It felt like maybe she had somehow sped up.

"I don't get it," said Kurt. "Should have started already. Don't know why I'm not seeing anything yet. Maybe there's a time dilation..."

Sandra felt herself rising from the chair. Broken glass

crunched underfoot as she approached the window. Cars were stopped in the middle of the street, the drivers out of their vehicles staring up into space. A man with blood gushing from a grotesquely dislocated shoulder picked himself up from under a truck's bumper and hobbled past.

She looked up at the sky. A comet would have been the closest description but that didn't really cut it. It seemed less a physical object than some kind of force or energy, like a magnetic disturbance, or more to her view, like a hole punched in the universe. It was coming on at what felt like a tremendous speed.

An explosion rocked the street below. She glanced down, saw a man enveloped in flames exit a truck to get a better look at the sky. She caught a whiff of diesel exhaust and burnt flesh before she lost interest and glanced back up.

The comet grew larger as it approached, a hazy purple-white sphere with a coal-black core. Around the comet the air shimmered and glowed red. There was a strange holographic quality to it that seemed to resist clear focus when viewed straight on, only forming into a distinct image on the backs of Sandra's eyelids when she blinked. The resulting impression was that of staring into a heavenly eye.

"Something's wrong..." Kurt's words were coming out deep and slow like a record player running out of power. "I don't know ....must have missed a decimal point..."

The comet had come to dominate the horizon. It seemed to have slowed, maybe even stopped, but Sandra felt her sense of time was no longer reliable. As the purple iris wrapped around her, the world falling away before its expanse, there was a sense of motion as though she were being drawn forward into the comet's heart. The distance between her and the core faded to nothing, then dissolved entirely.

It was an immersive blackness without form and void. A disjointed sensation of moving through the dark or it through her, like falling down a bottomless pit. A speed so fantastic that the horizon warped and flattened around her. At the furthest reaches a light emerged. Faint at first, then growing bright and divided from the darkness like a rift in the universe. She was being thrust towards it, through it. The beams refracted around her, the white beams turning crimson in her wake, pooling beneath her like a lake of fire. It was, she realized, not one light but all light. It was eternity, coming on at an overwhelming speed. In her last conscious thought, Sandra wondered if she were flying outward into infinity or falling inward to nothingness, and then all was dark again.

"…just…feel like such an ass…."

Sandra came to as though waking from a dream. She was lying outside on the fire escape, a crippling pain in her back. She placed a protective hand over her stomach. One story above her jagged shards of the office window. Somehow the other hand was still holding the phone.

"….a terrible mistake. I was obviously wrong about this whole thing. I don't know what to say, other than I'm so very sorry…"

"That's…ok," she mumbled.

"You're still there! Oh, thank God! I hadn't heard from you, I was afraid the call had dropped."

"Mmm."

"I was starting to panic. I was thinking, I don't know how I'm going to get off this ship if the phone dies. How anyone would ever find me out here. Anyway, if you could alert a rescue crew or something…"

The phone slipped out of Sandra's fingers and cracked open on the pavement three stories down. She stared up into the sky, the last purple glow of sunset fading on the horizon, the soundscape an oddly comforting mix of sirens, alarms, the crackle of fire. Her face felt raw and puffy, as though she'd been crying. It was important that she go to the doctor, get a full check-up, she told herself. But at that moment, lying there, all was calm, all was sensical. She felt great. Better than she had in a very long time.

Fabiana Elisa Martínez

Conversations

Among the many disadvantages of childhood, between the vulnerability of an immature brain and a completely open heart, there is a minuscule chip of gold that tints all and counteracts the naked ignorance of our early years: marvel. Until I was four and left the convent, marvel was more omnipresent around me than the bearded good god Sister Suzanna tried to instill in my incipient reasoning.

I marveled at the baby rabbits that balled themselves in burrows and came out bubbling around their mother when the school cat was far away. I was delighted by the thick chocolate my mother served me every morning that smelled like a diminutive fireplace inside a nutshell. Every act of nature, from the growth of my toenails to the whistling of the wind, was a reason to exist in awe.

Silence was also part of the elements that filled my young days with bliss. Not only the silence around me, framed by hushed slippers running to a service or the tingling of the milk bottles that the milkman left every morning on the stone kitchen counter without making my mom ever look at him. For a long time, I also believed that the nuns were mute like my mother and only sister Suzanna and I had the gift of singing, babbling, and laughing out loud when nobody could see us. I understood much later that the nuns were steered by a strange mechanism that allowed them to talk in intervals during the day, never stepping on each other's words, never interrupting the blessed one who one day a week should renounce to her nourishment to read the biblical passage at lunch or dinner.

Not only this silence, the exterior one, impregnated my days, my skipping shadow, and all the stars of Porto above me. There was my inner silence as well, my lack of questions. The dark side of marvel is the futility of asking, the tacit prohibition of questioning

64

either the falling of petals after a storm or the magical powers of the holy water in our little chapel.

I talked with sister Suzanna. We shared long conversations in her greenhouse. Our exchanges about worms, turtles, and spiders were always two simultaneous languages. Whenever she explained the world to me, she made her hands fly like butterflies and fluttered her fingers above her face and heart to signify exactly what she was saying in Portuguese. Later in life, still without asking, I learned that sister Suzanna and my grandmother had an unvoiced agreement. Sign language would help me communicate with my mother if she ever decided to talk to me.

I never asked sister Suzanna or the other nuns why my mother looked so sad. For me, that was the nature of the universe, the norm, the established order to which I had arrived at birth. My mom and I did not converse. We looked at each other, she traced my features with the tip of her finger every night in bed. She made for me the silky chocolate that poured into my cup like the wavy mane of a Portuguese mermaid. My mom cooked for the nuns and cleaned the school and the cloisters. She polished the gilded ornaments in the chapel before the morning mass. That was my world, tranquil and pure until I told Sister Romé she was too ugly to deserve a piece of my fourth birthday cake.

I remember the mumbling from behind the enormous wooden doors of Sister Romé's office. My mom was in the kitchen drying stubborn tears with her apron. Sister Suzanna sat beside me on the cold stone bench in the cloister waiting for my grandmother to exit. My favorite nun seemed nervous, less prone to talk than usual. I squeezed her hand and asked without raising my eyes, "Why is my grandmother here? She only comes in the heat."

"You mean in the summer?"

"I mean why is she here?"

"Because you will be going to Lisbon with her. You are a big girl now."

I bit my lower lip and heard inside my head a million pieces of glass showering down on merciless cobblestones like the day my mom dropped the holy wine carafe in the church after Sister Romé passed next to her whispering something about that girl of hers, the dirty fruit of her sin.

Sister Suzanna tightened my right braid and kissed me on the forehead while my grandmother checked her train tickets and the lock of my cardboard suitcase that contained more rag dolls and flower seeds than dresses and socks.

In the following years, as marvel withdrew from my world and my Portuguese and all the other languages my grandmother taught me flourished in my brain like the bunnies at the convent, I lost the signs that would have allowed a timid chat between an older me and my mother. I only remember crumbs of those wrist revolutions: love, tear, balloon, milk. I forgot the rest: mother, cat, stones, and love.

Nonfiction

Fatherhood

Tonight, the sound of breaking wood booms like thunder. It startles my older sister and me, and we run from the kitchen of our Long Island home to our living room window. We see our neighbor's teenage son and his three friends standing in a circle on their driveway. The boys' voices echo like a fever.

One of them holds a six-pack of Coors Light by its plastic rings. The group eggs him on, pushing him toward our front yard's rail and post fence and closer to a moment of decision. He's all in. He unleashes a karate-style kick that splits one of the wooden planks into two. The crunching and cracking remind me of a firework show's finale.

Jennifer, fourteen, opens our front door and screams, "Stop!"

Someone screams back, "Go inside!"

The boy does it again, this time more stomp than kick, and another plank breaks apart. Our fence, which separates our green front lawn from the dirt and daffodils of our neighbor's, lies in ruins.

At age ten, I boil with rage. When the boys go inside, I stride into the night. I cut across our lawn littered with shards of wood. I'm looking for something to break. I approach the neighbor's rusting, white mailbox, its cylinder-shaped metal canister attached to a pole in the ground. It becomes my target. I strike at its top with the bottoms of my fists. It comes off easily, falling with a thud onto the sidewalk.

I pick up the mailbox and cradle it as a barbaric prize.

On my return to the house, Jennifer watches me place the mailbox on our kitchen counter. She says, "You're being crazy." She tells me to return it. Instead, I pick it up again and carry it out our back door. Behind our property is a woodsy area we call "the sump," which begins with a sharp drop of several feet before expanding into rows of trees and wild brush. Dad constantly warns us never to go in there.

I stand by the six-foot-high fence that cordons off our backyard from this forbidden territory. Using two hands, I launch the mailbox into the air like it's a discus built for flight. It soars over the top of the fence. I hear it crash to the ground with a satisfying rattle.

"What did you just do?" Jennifer asks when I come back inside.

"I threw their mailbox into the sump." Her face tightens with dread. "It's gone," I say.

***

My father, with whom we've lived since the divorce, arrives home and notices the broken fence.

"What happened?"

"We saw the neighbors kicking it," my sister says. "We yelled, but they didn't stop."

My dad closes his mouth to contain the heat. I can't tell whether he's more angry about the broken fence or that we confronted our neighbors. Jennifer delivers the news about the mailbox. My father stares at me with eyes as hard as rocks.

I state my case. "They broke our fence on purpose. They were laughing about it!"

Dad is unmoved. "You can't just break people's mailboxes, Brad."

"Well, I did. And it's missing."

He screams, "What are you talking about?! Where is it?"

"I'm not telling."

Green veins bulge on his forehead like Bruce Banner before the turn. "You're going to tell me right now."

"Fine. I threw it over the backyard fence."

"Jesus Christ, Brad!"

My father makes me follow him to the backyard. He

makes me stand in the spot where I tossed the mailbox. He goes out our back gate, walks down a narrow passageway that runs between our house and the neighbor's, and enters the woods.

Leaves crackle under his feet. Beams of light from the flashlight he's brought for the search travel through tiny openings in the lattice fence. I picture my dad as a scavenging animal. I wish aloud that he never finds the mailbox.

But within minutes, he does. He walks past me, holding it under his right arm like a running back does a football.

"What are you doing, Dad?"

"I'm going to fix the mailbox."

It is past midnight when my father retrieves his toolbox from the garage. He walks into the chill of the fall evening toward our neighbor's property. Using pliers and a screwdriver, he works to reattach the canister to its pole.

I watch from our front porch. I mourn every turn of the screw that unsettles the score and signals our surrender. I want my father to go along with my act of revenge.

I want him to fight.

Years from now, I'll remember this as the moment my hero worship of Dad began to fade. That's how the memory will stand, frozen in disappointment for decades.

Then, I become a father.

Small Orchard Bearing Bones

On their way to the gravesite, the two Lake Charles cops keep their stride, but Corporal Bendy Falcon tightens his jaw. He has a bad feeling about this. Sergeant Chad Manuel grins and swings his left arm around his buddy's wide shoulders. Falcon looks down at his boots advancing through sodden grass dotted with crawfish chimneys, and shakes his head no.

I hadn't expected to call the police today. I'd spent the morning photographing the area as part of a research project, then pulled over to visit a cemetery where many of the people these streets were named after lay at rest. But soon after I arrived, I nearly tripped over a bone. Then another. I stepped back and saw the unmistakable arc of a femur bone resting on top of a crypt. I hesitated before dialing the police. Part of me felt I was trespassing—not just on land but on something deeper, a boundary between past and present, memory and neglect. I wasn't sure what I had stumbled into.

But now, as the officers and I stop at the first crypt before us, I'm relieved to have company. The bone rests on top of a crypt for John Cloud, who died in 1943, a day after Valentine's Day and a month before his 86th birthday. The bone is graceful, a shocking white against gray cement covering a crumbling masonry crypt. It's been recently gnawed by an animal, and a few flakes cling to the bone and below its fine arc on the rain wet cement.

"Where did you find this?" Falcon asks. He isn't looking at the bone or me.

"Right here," I say, motioning toward the crypt. "The ground is so soft from rain, bones are just…coming loose."

Sergeant Manuel squats, shining his Maglite into an open corner of the crypt. "How many?"

"A lot," I say. "That's why I called."

Falcon is creeped out, and now there's rising outrage. "It's open! Wide open!" He steps back and swings his head toward Goos

Street to look around the cemetery. Rain has been sprinkling off and on all afternoon from dense, leaden clouds.

Manuel shines his Maglite into a hole left by fallen cornerstone bricks that someone has stacked on top of the crypt. "There's a body in there."

The crypt is spacious, dusty. About the size of a twin bed, bigger than a double bathtub. A skull rests at the top, under where the headstone is. Its mandible seems to be missing. Below, ribs scatter like slender petals of a white flower or waning half-moons, like long lunulae of clasped fingers. Slim arm bones lay askew. Under a filament that flickers from a crack in the crypt, the flashlight halo strikes sturdy leg bones.

Falcon doesn't look. Underneath his high and tight haircut, his neck is tense. "They list 'em in the paper. Have you seen, in the paper? They list names and relatives who are supposed to maintain 'em."

Thirty feet down the mushy cemetery grounds, the sides of a masonry crypt have collapsed. Under bricks and a couple rusted support braces, femur bones, chalky white. Nearby, in a cinderblock crypt, white chips like oyster shells pillow what appears to be a pubic bone. Inside another crumbling cinderblock crypt, planks of a coffin have been pulled aside. A few bones remain, but with the exception of John Cloud's, there are no skulls visible in any of the open crypts.

Deep tire tracks make clear the cemetery is regularly mowed and there's some litter. An empty pint of Classic Cask whiskey is on top of one grave marker near Goos Street. Some crypts have been maintained recently. Nylon red roses wired to a white plastic angel have faded to russet, but they're still whole, spiked to the ground in memory of someone whose crypt is open in the back. Inside, a potato chip bag lay among scattered bones.

S.T. Goosby's crypt is intact. On top of a marble headstone is an oval-shaped ceramic picture of the deceased, a Black man with a pyramidal mustache, black tie, white handkerchief in the pocket of a black suit jacket. Under the dates that spanned his life—1900 to

1946—his reputation is carved: "He had a smile and good word for everyone." His friendly expression corroborates the carver's claim.

One crypt bears an inscription handwritten at burial. On the east-facing panel where the feet of her loved one were laid to rest, someone spread cement, then wrote in large simple print: "ALICE HAWKINS 3rd 5 1961." The carved marble headstone atop the crypt identifies the dead as Alice Hackett, born 1877.

Sergeant Manuel isn't sure who to call. But Falcon's dread is in the muscled clutch of his anger. His forehead bunches like a crushed can. He might have had a better day if he didn't know about this. Making his way back to the curb, he grumbles to his boots steadily punching a path to his squad car. "I told my father, cremate me and sprinkle it in the garden. He said that'll make the vegetables taste bad."

I linger a moment longer, looking over the cemetery, at the names I had come here to study. I had wanted to give shape to stories buried beneath the ground. But history isn't neat, and neither is memory. The past pushes through the cracks, demanding to be seen.

Falcon doesn't look back. He keeps his eyes on the wet pavement ahead, stepping carefully, as if avoiding something no one else can see. Behind him, the rain darkens the bones one by one.

At the end of the street, Bourque Smith Woodard Memorials LLC displays an assortment of marble headstones behind a large yellow sign with a double black arrow: "Traffic goes both ways."

Blue-Eyed Doe

The old home video shot 7 years ago. One person is sitting in the chair, purple slippers on their feet. Those were the slippers with the white puff balls at the top. The sliding glass door is open. That let in the ocean air. Another person is talking to the baby. They're filming with my camera. That camera I got from them. There are birthday decorations everywhere. Green dinosaurs and presents (cars, trucks, toys) and a cake in the kitchen. Presents have already been open. The baby is being filmed. Someone else picks up the baby. I walk into view of the camera and talk to the person behind it. Everyone in this video is dead now. Besides myself. And the baby.

Contributors

Sherry Abaldo's writing has appeared or is forthcoming in *The New York Times, ONE ART, Rattle, Sequestrum, The Mackinaw, Eunoia Review, Down East Magazine,* and on The History Channel and PBS among other outlets. As a professional researcher, her latest contribution is due from William Morrow in November 2025, a sweeping nonfiction World War II story called *The Dangerous Shore.* Born and raised in rural Maine, she currently lives in Las Vegas with her husband. More at www.sherryabaldo.com.

Maria Berardi's poems appear online, in print, in university journals, meditation magazines, newspapers, and art galleries. She can be reached at maria-berardi.com.

Emma Bolden is the author of a memoir, *The Tiger and the Cage: A Memoir of a Body in Crisis* (Soft Skull), and the poetry collections *House Is an Enigma, medi(t)ations,* and *Maleficae.* Her work has appeared in such journals as *Ploughshares, The Gettysburg Review, New England Review, Seneca Review, Pleiades, Prairie Schooner, TriQuarterly,* and *Shenandoah.* The recipient of an NEA Fellowship, she is an editor of *Screen Door Review: Literary Voices of the Queer South.*

Acie Clark is a writer from Florida and Georgia. He received his MFA from the University of Alabama where he worked for *Black Warrior Review* as the online editor. He teaches in the Film, Theatre, and Creative Writing Department at the University of Central Arkansas and as a summer instructor at Interlochen Center for the Arts. He is a 2024-2025 Fine Arts Work Center fellow in poetry. His recent work can be found or is forthcoming in *Shenandoah, Passages North,* and *Arkansas International.*

Originally from Los Angeles, **Susan Cobin** now lives in Lexington, KY. She has published poems in dozens of literary magazines, including *The Malahat Review, Kayak, Poetry East, Permafrost, Cimarron Review,* and *Michigan Quarterly Review,* and short fiction in *Allium, a Journal of Poetry and Prose.* Her poetry collection, *What You Choose,* was published by Broadstone Books.

Stasha Cole is a PhD student in literature at The University of Tulsa. Her work is forthcoming in *Zaum, Anodyne,* and others. She is the editorial assistant at *Nimrod International Journal.*

Whitney Cooper is a poet from Columbus, Georgia. Their work appears in *Glassworks Magazine, Stillpoint Literary Magazine, Calliope, Right Hand Pointing,* and *SHARK REEF.* Their hobbies include writing, painting, and amateur birding. They live in metro Atlanta with their wife and two beasts, Socks and Louie.

Frank Foster is a published author in the world of commercial real estate economics; as a nonfiction writer, his next publication will be his first. He lives in Cambridge, Massachusetts.

Jan Freeman is the author of three books of poetry, most recently *Blue Structure,* and a new manuscript of poems, *The Odyssey of Yes and No.* Among her many awards are MacDowell fellowships, a Spiral Shell Fellowship at Moulin a Nef, and VCCA fellowships. Her poems have appeared in *Poetry, North American Review, Barrow Street, Plume, Salamander, the Brooklyn Rail, Tar River Poetry, American Poetry Review,* and other journals. She is the founder and former director of Paris Press and teaches ekphrastic poetry workshops and the MASS MoCA Writing Through Art Poetry Retreats. www.janfreeman.net.

Emma Grey Rose is a writer based in San Diego, California from Portland, Oregon. Her work has appeared in *Frighten the Horses, Spinozablue, Iceblink Lit, Sodapop Press,* and elsewhere. She is the author of *All The Beautiful Things* (Midsummer Dream House, 2024).

Max Gutmann has contributed to *Able Muse, Measure, THINK,* and other journals and magazines.

Caleb Jagoda is a poet, journalist, and MFA candidate at the University of New Hampshire. He is managing editor at *Barnstorm Journal* and his work has appeared in *Polaris Literary Magazine, Write on the DOT,* and *Down East Magazine.* He lives in Dover, New Hampshire.

Emma Johnson-Rivard is a midwestern writer of poetry and weird fiction. Her work has appeared in *Strange Horizons, Coffin Bell, Moon City Review,* and others. She can be found at Bluesky at @blackcattales and at emmajohnson-rivard.com.

Katrina Kaye is a writer and educator living in Albuquerque, NM. She is seeking an audience for her ever-growing surplus of poetic meanderings. Find her hoard of previously published writing on her website: poetkatrinakaye.com. She is grateful to anyone who reads her work and in awe of those willing to share it.

Zach Keali'i Murphy is a Hawaii-born writer with a background in cinema. His stories appear in *Raritan Quarterly, The MacGuffin, Reed Magazine, The Coachella Review, Another Chicago Magazine, Bamboo Ridge, Flash Frog,* and more. He has published the chapbook *Tiny Universes* (Selcouth Station Press). He lives with his wonderful wife, Kelly, in St. Paul, Minnesota.

Megan Leonard (she/they) is the author of *Book of Lullabies* (Milk & Cake Press, 2020) and *Larkspur Queen* (Broadstone Books, 2025).

Alison Luterman's four books of poems include *The Largest Possible Life; See How We Almost Fly; Desire Zoo;* and *In the Time of Great*

Fires. She has published poems in *The New York Times Magazine,*
*The Sun Magazine, Prairie Schooner, Nimrod, Rattle, The Atlanta
Review, Main Street Rag,* among others. Two of her poems are
included in Billy Collins' Poetry 180 project at the Library of
Congress. Five of her personal essays have been collected in the
e-book *Feral City.* www.alisonluterman.net

Josh Mahler lives and writes in Virginia. His poems have
appeared in *Denver Quarterly, Tar River Poetry, Quarter After
Eight, South Dakota Review, The Louisville Review, The Carolina
Quarterly, Valparaiso Poetry Review, Potomac Review, The Southern
Poetry Anthology,* from Texas Review Press, and elsewhere.

Fabiana Elisa Martínez authored the short story collections *12
Random Words* and *Conquered by Fog,* and the grammar *Spanish
360 with Fabiana.* Other stories of hers were published
in *Rigorous Magazine, The Closed Eye Open, Ponder Review, The
Halcyone, Hindsight Magazine, Libretto Magazine,* and the
anthology *Writers of Tomorrow.*

David Matthews is a native of the South Carolina Midlands,
poet, runner, resident of Portland, Oregon. Poems have appeared
in *Adelaide Literary Magazine, Quill & Parchment, Steam
Ticket, Ghost Town Poetry Vol. Two,* and other publications. He
writes about politics and current affairs as conscience and honest
indignation dictate, and about literary and intellectual matters as
the spirit moves, at David Matthews Portable Bohemia (https://
davidmatthewsportablebohemia.substack.com/).

Michelle McMillan-Holifield is a Best of the Net and Pushcart
nominee. She pens poetry, book reviews, fiction, and creative nonfiction. Her work has been included in or is forthcoming in *Boxcar
Poetry Review, Nelle, Sky Island Journal, Stirring, The Collagist, The
Main Street Rag, Whale Road Review,* and *Windhover,* among others.
She hopes you one day find her poetry tacked to a tree somewhere
in the Alaskan Wild.

Michael Milburn teaches English in New Haven, Connecticut. He has published poems and essays recently in *Avenue, Third Wednesday, Chicago Quarterly Review,* and *Salmagundi.*

Mark J. Mitchell has been a working poet for 50 years. He's the author of five full-length collections, and six chapbooks. His latest collection is *Something To Be* from Pski's Porch Publishing. He's fond of baseball, Louis Aragon, Dante, and his wife, activist Joan Juster. He lives in San Francisco where he points out pretty things.

Steve Parker is a new writer with two modest pieces published in literary magazines.

Andrea Potos is the author of several collections of poetry, most recently *Her Joy Becomes* (Fernwood Press), *Two Emilys,* and *Marrow of Summer,* both from Kelsay Books. Another collection, *The Presence of One Word,* is forthcoming from Fernwood Press in 2025. Andrea's poems appear widely in print and online, including most recently in *Paterson Literary Review, Rosebud, Poetry East, Poem, Midwest Quarterly, One Art, The Sun,* and others. She lives in Madison, Wisconsin.

Ron Riekki has been awarded a 2014 Michigan Notable Book, 2015 The Best Small Fictions, 2016 Shenandoah Fiction Prize, 2016 IPPY Award, 2019 Red Rock Film Fest Award, 2019 Best of the Net finalist, 2019 Très Court International Film Festival Audience Award and Grand Prix, 2020 Dracula Film Festival Vladutz Trophy, 2020 Rhysling Anthology inclusion, and 2022 Pushcart Prize. Right now, Riekki's listening to LCD Soundsystem's "Someone Great."

Cliff Saunders is the author of several poetry chapbooks, including *Mapping the Asphalt Meadows* (Slipstream Publications) and *The Persistence of Desire* (Kindred Spirit Press). His poems have appeared recently in *Quadrant, The Rockford Review, Gigantic Tentacles, Bare Hill Review,* and *Little Leaf Literary Journal.*

Nina Schuyler's short story collection, *In This Ravishing World*, won the W.S. Porter Prize and the Prism Prize for Climate Literature and was published in July 2024. Her novel, *Afterword*, won the 2024 PenCraft Book of the Year in Fiction, the Foreword INDIES Book of the Year Award for Science Fiction and Literary, and the PenCraft Spring Seasonal Book Award for Literary and Science Fiction. Her short stories have been published by *Zyzzyva*, *Chicago Quarterly Review*, *Nashville Review*, and elsewhere, and have been nominated for a Pushcart Prize. She teaches creative writing for Stanford Continuing Studies and Book Passage.

Brad Snyder's writing has appeared or is forthcoming in *HuffPost Personal*, *River Teeth's Beautiful Things*, *Sweet Lit*, *Under the Gum Tree*, *The Gay & Lesbian Review*, and elsewhere. He holds an MFA in Creative Nonfiction Writing from Bay Path University. Find more of his work at bradmsnyder.com and Medium @bradmsnyder.

Jeffery Allen Tobin is a political scientist and researcher based in South Florida. He has been writing for more than 30 years. His latest poetry collection, *Scars & Fresh Paint*, was published in 2024, and his poetry, prose, and essays have been featured in many journals, magazines, and websites.

Kerry Trautman is a lifelong Ohioan whose work has appeared in various anthologies and journals. Her one-act play, "Mass," was a winner of The Toledo Repertoire Theater's "Toledo Voices" competition, and it will receive a stage reading in 2025. Her books are *Things That Come in Boxes* (King Craft Press, 2012), *To Have Hoped* (Finishing Line Press, 2015), *Artifacts* (NightBallet Press, 2017), *To be Nonchalantly Alive* (Kelsay Books, 2020), *Marilyn: Self-Portrait, Oil on Canvas* (Gutter Snob Books, 2022), *Unknowable Things* (Roadside Press, 2022), and *Irregulars* (Stanchion Books, 2023).

Suzanne Underwood Rhodes is the Arkansas Poet Laureate and the author of six poetry collections, the most recent a chapbook, *The Perfume of Pain.* Her second full collection, *Flying Yellow,* was named a semi-finalist in the North American Book Award. She has recent work in *Dappled Things, Spiritus, Southern Voices: 50 Contemporary Poets,* and *Slant.* She brings "Poetry on Purpose" to dementia patients in a memory care center and taught poetry to formerly incarcerated women at Magdalene Serenity House in Fayetteville. A retired college instructor, she teaches virtual poetry workshops at the Muse Writers Center in Norfolk, Virginia, as well as at schools and universities throughout Arkansas.

Cesca Janece Waterfield is a writer, oral historian, and chionophile. Her work has appeared in *The Comstock Review, Scalawag Magazine, Mystery Tribune, Deep South Magazine, LUMINA,* and more. Her poetry collections include *Conspiracy Cherry* (Ludic Arts) and *The Oyster Garden* (Selene Pressworks). She is passionate about oral history as a way to document voices that might otherwise go unheard, and about using storytelling to explore the intersections of personal experience and social change. She received her MFA in Creative Writing and MA in Literature at McNeese State University.

Daniel Weiss is a writer, archaeologist, and ceramicist originally from River Forest, IL. He earned his B.A. in anthropology from Kenyon College in 2024 and has since worked as an archaeologist. At Kenyon, he helped found, curated, and produced layout for the college's newest literary magazine. He also produced layout for the college's oldest student-run literary magazine and reviewed submissions for the *Kenyon Review* for two years. As an archaeologist, he cherishes the opportunity to meet the past in person. He lets this experience, along with its inherent relationship to nature and the passage of time, inform his work.

Angelina Weld Grimké (1880-1958) was a trailblazing African American poet and dramatist of the Harlem Renaissance. Descended from prominent abolitionists, her lyrical work explored themes of racial justice and personal identity. Her groundbreaking play, "Rachel," (1916) was among the first to confront lynching for mainstream audiences. Grimké's recently rediscovered poetry, much unpublished in her lifetime, establishes her as an early queer voice in African American literature, whose delicate yet powerful verse continues to resonate today.

Yvonne Zipter (1954-2025) is the author of the poetry collections *The Wordless Lullaby of Crickets, Kissing the Long Face of the Greyhound, The Patience of Metal,* and *Like Some Bookie God.* Her published poems are currently being sold individually in Chicago in two repurposed toy-vending machines, the proceeds of which are donated to the nonprofit arts organization Arts Alive Chicago. She is also the author of the nonfiction books *Diamonds Are a Dyke's Best Friend* and *Ransacking the Closet* and the Russian historical novel *Infraction.*